THE FATE
OF A MAN

MIKHAIL SHOLOKHOV

Fredonia Books
Amsterdam, The Netherlands

The Fate of a Man

by
Mikhail Sholokhov

ISBN: 1-4101-0424-9

Reprinted from the 1957 edition

Fredonia Books
Amsterdam, The Netherlands
http://www.fredoniabooks.com

*For Yevgenia Grigoryevna Levitskaya
Member of the C.P.S.U. since 1903*

There was a rare drive and swiftness in the first spring that came to the upper reaches of the Don in the first year after the war. At the end of March, warm winds blew from the shores of the Azov Sea and in two days the sands on the left bank of the river were bare, the snow-choked gullies and ravines swelled in the steppe, the streams burst the ice and flooded madly and the roads became almost completely impassable.

At this unfavourable time of the year it so happened that I had to make a journey to the district centre of Bukanovskaya. The distance was not great—only about sixty kilometres—but it turned out to be hard going. My friend and I set out before sunrise. The pair of well-fed horses strained at the traces and could scarcely pull the heavy wagon. The wheels sank axle-deep into the damp mush of sand mixed with snow and ice and in an hour creamy white flecks of foam appeared on the horses' flanks and under the narrow straps of the breech bands, and the fresh morning air was filled with the sharp intoxicating smell of horses' sweat and warm harness lavishly smeared with tar.

Where the going was particularly heavy for the horses we got out and walked. The slushy snow squelched under our boots and it was hard to get along, but the roadside was still coated with a glittering crust of ice, and there it was even harder. It took us about six hours to do the thirty kilometres as far as the ford over the River Yelanka.

The little river at Mokhovskoi village, almost dry in summer, had now flooded over a full kilometre of marshy alder-grown water meadows. We had to make the crossing in a leaky flat-bottomed boat that could not take more than three people at the most. We sent the horses back. In a collective-farm shed on the other side an old and battered jeep that had been standing there all the winter was awaiting us. The driver and I with some misgivings climbed into the unsteady little craft. My friend stayed behind on the bank with our things. We had scarcely pushed off when little fountains of water came spouting up through the rotten planks. We plugged them with anything we could lay hands on and kept bailing until we reached the other side. In an hour we were on the far bank of the river. The driver fetched the jeep from the village and went back to the boat.

"If this perishing old tub doesn't fall to bits in the water," he said, picking up an oar, "I'll be back with your friend in a couple of hours. At the earliest."

The village lay a good distance from the river, and down by the water there was that kind of stillness that falls on deserted places only in the depths of autumn or at the very beginning of spring. The water gave off a damp smell mingled with the tart bitterness of rotting alders, and from the distant steppes bathing in a lilac haze of mist a light breeze brought the eternally young, barely perceptible aroma of earth that has not long been liberated from the snow.

Not far away, on the sand at the water's edge, lay a broken wattle fence. I sat down on it to have a smoke but, on putting my hand in my jacket pocket, discovered to my great disappointment that the packet of cigarettes I had been carrying there was soaked. On the way across a wave had slapped over the side of the wallowing boat and drenched me to the waist in muddy water. There had been no time to think of my cigarettes, for I had to drop my oar and start bailing as fast as I could to save us from sinking, but now, vexed at my own carelessness, I drew the sodden packet gingerly out of my pocket, got down on my haunches and began laying out the moist brownish cigarettes one by one on the fence.

It was noon. The sun shone as hot as in May. I hoped the cigarettes would soon dry. It was so hot that I began to regret having put on my quilted army trousers and jacket for the journey. It was the first really warm day of the year. But it was good to sit there alone, abandoning myself completely to the stillness and solitude, and, taking off my old army *ushanka*, to let the breeze dry my hair after the heavy work of rowing, and to stare up vacantly at the big-breasted clouds floating in the faded blue.

Presently I noticed a man come out on the road from behind the end cottages of the village. He was leading a little boy, about five or six years old, I reckoned, not more. They tramped wearily towards the ford, but, on reaching the jeep, turned and came in my direction. The man, tall and rather stooped, came right up to me and said in a deep husky voice:

"Hullo, mate."

"Hullo." I shook the big rough hand he offered me.

The man bent down to the little boy and said: "Say hullo to Uncle, lad. Looks as if he's another driver like your dad. Only you and I used to drive a lorry, didn't we, and he goes about in that little bus over there."

Looking straight at me with a pair of eyes that were as bright and clear as the sky, and smiling a little, the boy boldly held out a pink cold hand. I shook it gently and asked: "Feeling chilly, old man? Why's your hand so cold on a hot day like this?"

With a touching childish trustfulness the boy pressed against my knees and lifted his little flaxen eyebrows in surprise.

"But I'm not an old man, Uncle. I'm only a boy, and I'm not chilly either. My hands are just cold because I've been making snowballs."

Taking the half-empty rucksack off his back, the father sat down heavily beside me and said: "This passenger of mine is a regular young nuisance, he is. He's made me tired as

7

well as himself. If you take a long stride he breaks into a trot; just you try keeping in step with a footslogger like him. Where I could take one pace, I have to take three instead, and so we go on, like a horse and a tortoise. And you need eyes in the back of your head to know what he's doing. As soon as you turn your back, he's off paddling in a puddle or breaking off an icicle and sucking it like a lollipop. No, it's no job for a man to be travelling with someone like him, not on foot anyway." He was silent for a little, then asked: "And what about you, mate, waiting for your chief?"

By now I didn't want to tell him I was not a driver, so I answered:

"Looks as if I'll have to."

"Is he coming over from the other side?"

"He will be."

"Do you know if the boat will be here soon?"

"In about two hours' time."

"That's a fair stretch. Well, let's have a rest, I'm in no hurry. Just saw you as I was walking past, so I thought to myself there's one of us, drivers, taking a spot of sunshine. I'll go over and have a smoke with him, I thought. No fun in smoking alone, any more than in dying alone. You live well, I see, smoking cigarettes. Got them wet, eh? Well, brother, wet tobacco's like a doctored horse, neither of them any good. Let's have a go at my old shag instead."

He pulled a worn silk pouch out of the pocket of his thin khaki trousers, and as he unrolled it, I noticed the words embroidered on the corner: "To one of our dear soldiers from a pupil of Lebedyanskaya Secondary School."

We smoked the strong home-grown tobacco and for a long time neither of us spoke. I was going to ask him where he was making for with the boy, and what brought him out on such bad roads, but he got his question in first:

"At it all through the war, were you?"

"Nearly all of it."

"Front line?"

"Yes."

"Well, I had a good bellyful of trouble out there too, mate, more than enough of it."

He rested his big dark hands on his knees and let his shoulders droop. When I glanced at him sideways I felt strangely disturbed. Have you ever seen eyes that look as if they've been sprinkled with ash, eyes filled with such ingrained yearning and sadness that it is hard to look into them? This chance acquaintance of mine had eyes like that.

He broke a dry twisted twig out of the fence and for a minute traced a curious pattern in the sand with it, then he spoke:

"Sometimes I can't sleep at night, I just stare into the darkness and I think: 'What did you do it for, life, why did you maim me like this? Why did you tear the guts out of me?' And I get no answer, either in darkness, or when the sun's shining bright.... No, I get no answer, and I'll never get one!" And suddenly he recollected himself, nudged his little son affectionately and said: "Go on, laddie, go and play down by the water, there's always something for little boys to do by a big river. Only mind you don't get your feet wet."

While we had been smoking together in silence, I had taken a quick look at father and son and one thing about them had struck me as unusual. The boy was dressed plainly but in good stout clothes. The way the long-skirted little coat with its soft lining of worn beaver lamb fitted him, the way his tiny boots had been made to fit snugly over the woollen socks, the very neat darn that joined an old tear on the sleeve of the coat, all these things spoke of a woman's hand, the skilful hand of a mother. But the father's appearance was different. His quilted jacket was scorched in several places and roughly darned, the patch on his worn khaki trousers was not sewn on properly, it was tacked on with big mannish stitches; he was wearing an almost new pair of army shoes, but his thick woollen socks were full of holes. They had never known the touch of a woman's hand.... Even then I had thought, either he's a widower, or there's something wrong between him and his wife.

He watched his son run down to the water, then coughed and again began to speak, and I listened with all my attention.

"To start with, my life was just ordinary. I'm from the Voronezh Province, born there in 1900. During the Civil War I was in the Red Army, in Kikvidze's division. In the famine of 'twenty-two I struck out for the Kuban and worked like an ox for the kulaks, wouldn't be alive today if I hadn't. But my whole family back home, father, mother and sister, died of starvation. So I was left alone. As for relatives anywhere, I hadn't got a single one, not a soul. Well, after a year I came back from the Kuban, sold my cottage and went to Voronezh. First I worked as a carpenter, then I went to a factory and learned to be a mechanic. And soon I got married. My wife had been brought up in a children's home. She was an orphan. Yes, I got a good one there! Good-tempered, cheerful, always anxious to please. And smart she was, too, no comparison with me. She had known what real trouble was since she was a kid, mebbe that had an effect on her character. Just looking at her from the side, as you might say, she wasn't all that striking, but, you see, I wasn't looking at her from the side, I was looking at her full face. And for me there was no more beautiful woman in the whole world, and there never will be.

"I'd come home from work tired, and bad-tempered as hell sometimes. But no, she'd never fling your rudeness back at you. She'd be so gentle and quiet, couldn't do enough for you, always trying to get you a bit of something nice, even when there wasn't enough to go round. It made your heart lighter just to look at her, and after a while you'd put your arm round her and say: 'I'm sorry I was rude to you, Irina dear, I had a rotten day at work today.' And again there'd be peace between us, and my mind would be at rest. And you know what that means to your work, mate? In the morning I'd be out of bed like a shot and off to the factory, and any job I laid hands on would go like clockwork. That's what it means to have a real clever friend for a wife.

"Sometimes it'd happen that I'd have a drink with the boys on pay-day. And sometimes, the scissor-legged way I staggered home afterwards, it must have been frightening to watch. The main street wasn't wide enough for me, let alone the side streets. In those days I was a tough strong young fellow and I could hold a lot of drink, and I always got home on my own. But sometimes the last stretch would be in bottom gear, you know, I'd finish up by crawling on my hands and knees. But again I'd never get a word of reproach, no scolding, no shouting. My Irina, she'd just laugh at me, and she did that careful like so that even drunk as I was I wouldn't take it wrong. She'd pull my boots off and whisper: 'You'd better lie next to the wall tonight, Andrei, or you might fall out of bed in your sleep.' And I'd just flop down like a sack of oats and everything would go swimming round in front of me. And as I dropped off to sleep, I'd feel her stroking my head softly and whispering kind words, and I knew she felt sorry for me. . . .

"In the morning she'd get me up about two hours before work to give me time to come

13

round. She knew I wouldn't eat anything after being drunk, so she'd get me a pickled cucumber or something like that, and pour me out a good glass of vodka to take off the after-effects. 'Here you are, Andrei, but don't do it any more, dear.' How could a man let someone down who put such trust in him? I'd drink it up, thank her without words, just with a look and a kiss, and go off to work like a lamb. But if she'd had a word to say against me when I was drunk, if she'd started cursing or scolding me, I'd have come home drunk again, God's truth I would. That's what happens in some families where the wife's a fool. I've seen plenty of it and I know.

"Well, soon the children started arriving. First my little son was born, then two girls. And that was when I broke away from my mates. I started taking all my pay home to the wife; we had a fair-sized family now, and there was no time for drinking. On my day off I'd have just a glass of beer and let it go at that.

"In 'twenty-nine I got interested in motors, I learned to drive and started to work on a lorry. And when I got into the way of it I didn't want to go back to the factory any more. I found it more to my liking at the wheel. And so I lived for ten years without noticing how the time went by. It was like a dream. But what's ten years? Ask any man over forty if he's noticed how he's spent his life. You'll find he hasn't noticed a darned thing! The past is like that distant steppe way out there in the haze. This morning I was crossing it and it was clear all round, but now I've covered twenty kilometres there's a haze over it, and you can't tell the trees from the grass, nor the ploughland from the meadow.

"Those ten years I worked day and night. I earned good money and we lived no worse than other folk. And the children were a joy to us. All three did well at school, and the eldest, Anatoly, turned out to be so bright at mathematics that he even got his name in a Moscow newspaper. Where he inherited this great gift from, I couldn't tell you, mate. But it was a very nice thing for me, and I was proud of him, mighty proud I was!

"In ten years we saved up a bit of money and before the war we built ourselves a little cottage with two rooms and a shed and a little porch. Irina bought a couple of goats. What more did we want? There was milk for the children's porridge, we had a roof over our heads, clothes on our backs, shoes on our feet, so everything was all right. The only thing was I didn't choose a very good place to build. They allotted me a plot of land not far from an aircraft factory. Mebbe, if my little place had been somewhere else, my life would have turned out different....

"And then it came—war. The next day I had my call-up papers, and the day after it was, 'report to the station, please.' All my four saw me off together: Irina, Anatoly, and my daughters, Nastenka and Olyushka. The kids took it fine, though the girls couldn't keep back a tear or two. Anatoly just shivered a bit as if he was cold, he was getting on for seventeen by that time. But that Irina of mine.... I'd never seen anything like it in all the seventeen years we'd lived together. That night my shirt and chest were wet with her tears, and in the morning it was the same tale. We got to the station and I felt so sorry for her I couldn't look her in the face. Her lips were all swollen with tears, her hair was poking out from under her shawl, and her eyes were dull and staring like someone who's out of his mind. The officers gave the order to get aboard but she flung herself on my chest, and clasped her hands round my neck, and she was shaking all over, like a tree that's being chopped down.... The children tried to talk her round, and so did I, but nothing would help. Other women chatted to their husbands and sons, but mine clung to me like a leaf to a branch, and just trembled all the time, and couldn't say a word. 'Take a grip of yourself, Irina dear,' I said. 'Say something to me before I go, at least.' And this is what she said, with a sob between every word: 'Andrei ... my darling ... we'll never ... never see each other again ... in this world....'

"There was I with my heart bursting with pity for her, and she says a thing like that to me. She ought to have understood it wasn't easy for me to part with her, I wasn't going off to a party either. And that got my rag out! I pulled her hands apart and gave her a push. It seemed only a gentle push to me, but I was strong as an ox and she staggered back about three paces, then came towards me again with little steps, and I shouted at her: 'Is that the way to say good-bye? Do you want to bury me before my time?!' But then I took her in my arms again because I could see she was in a bad way...."

He broke off suddenly and in the silence that followed I heard a choking sound coming from his throat. His emotion communicated itself to me. I glanced sideways at him but did not see a single tear in those dead ashy eyes of his. He sat with his head drooping dejectedly. The big hands hanging limply at his sides were shaking slightly; his chin trembled, and so did his firm lips.

"Don't let it get you down, friend, don't think of it," I said quietly, but he seemed not to hear my words, and overcoming his emotion with a great effort, said suddenly in a hoarse, strangely altered voice:

"Till my last, dying day, till the last hour of my life I'll never forgive myself for pushing her away like that!"

He fell silent again and for a long time. He tried to roll a cigarette, but the strip of newspaper tore apart in his fingers and the tobacco scattered on to his knees. In the end he managed to make a clumsy roll of paper and tobacco, took a few hungry pulls at it, then, clearing his throat, went on:

"I tore myself away from Irina, took her face in my hands, and kissed her, and her lips were like ice. I said good-bye to the kids and ran to the carriage, managed to jump on the steps as it was moving. The train started off very slow, and it took me past my family again. I could see my poor little orphaned kids bunched up together, waving their hands and trying to smile, but not managing it. And Irina had her hands clasped to her breast, her lips as white as chalk, and she was whispering something, and staring, and her body was all bent forward as if she was trying to walk against a strong wind. And that's how I'll see her in my memory for the rest of my life--her hands clasped to her breast, those white lips, and her eyes wide open and full of tears. ... And that's mostly how I see her in my dreams too. Why did I push her away like that? Even now, when I remember, it's like a blunt knife twisting in my heart.

"We were drafted to our units at Belaya Tserkov, in the Ukraine. I was given a three-tonner, and that's what I went to the front in. Well, there's no point in telling you about the war, you saw it yourself and you know what it was like to start with. You'd get a lot of letters from home, but didn't write much yourself. Just now and then you'd write that everything was all right and you were doing a bit of fighting. Mebbe we're retreating at present, you'd say, but it won't be long before we gather our strength and give the Fritzies something to think about. And what else could you write? Those were grim times and you didn't feel like writing. And I must say I was never much of a one for harping on a pitiful note, and I couldn't stick the sight of those slobbering types that wrote to their wives and kids every day for no reason at all, just to rub their snot over the paper—oh, it's such a hard life, oh, I might get killed! And so he goes on, the son-of-a-bitch, complaining and looking for sympathy, blubbering away, and he can't understand that those poor unhappy women and kids are having just as bad a time of it back home as we are. Why, they were carrying the whole country on their shoulders. And what shoulders our women and children must have had not to be crushed down under a weight like that! But they weren't crushed, they stuck it out! And then one of those whimperers writes his pitiful letter and that just knocks a working woman off her feet. After a letter like that, the poor thing won't know what to do with herself or how to face up to her work. No! That's what a man's for, that's what you're a soldier for—to put up with everything, to bear everything, if need be. But if you've got more woman than man in you, then go and put on a frilled skirt to puff out your skinny arse, so you can look like a woman at least from behind, and go and weed the beet, or milk the cows, because your kind aren't needed at the front, the stink's bad enough there without you!

"But I didn't get even a year's fighting done.... I was wounded twice, but only slightly both times, once in the arm, the second time in the leg. The first was a bullet from an aircraft, the second a chunk of shrapnel. The Germans holed my lorry, top and sides, but I was lucky, mate, at first. I was lucky all the time, and then I was unlucky.... I got taken prisoner at Lozovenki in the May of 'forty-two. It was an awkward set-up. The Germans were attacking hard and one of our 120 mm. howitzer batteries had nearly run out of ammo; we loaded up my lorry chock-full of shells, I worked on the job myself till my shirt was sticking to my back. We had to get a move on because they were closing in on us; on the left we could hear a rumble of tanks, and firing on the right and in front, and things didn't smell too healthy.

" 'Can you get through, Sokolov?' asks the commander of our company. He need never have asked. Was I going to sit twiddling my thumbs while my mates got killed? 'What are you talking about!' I told him. 'I've got to get through, and that's that.' 'Get cracking then,' he says, 'and step on it.'

"And step on it I did. Never driven like that before in my life! I knew I wasn't carrying a load of spuds, I knew I had to be careful with the stuff I'd got aboard, but how could I be, when the lads were fighting out there empty-handed, when the whole road was under artillery fire. I did about six kilometres and got pretty near the place. I'd have to turn off the road to get to the hollow where the battery was stationed, and then what did I see? Strike me, if it wasn't our infantry running back across the field on both sides of the road with shells bursting all round them. What was I to do? I couldn't turn back, could I? So I gave her all she'd got. There was only about a kilometre to go to the battery, I had already turned off the road, but I never reached it, mate.... Must have been a long-range gun landed a heavy one near the lorry. I never heard the bang nor anything, just something burst inside my head, and I don't remember any more. How I stayed alive, and how long I lay there by the ditch, I've got no idea. I opened my eyes, but I couldn't get up; my head kept jerking and I was shaking as if I had a fever, everything seemed dark, something was scraping and grinding in my left shoulder, and my body ached all over as if somebody had been lamming into me for two days running with anything he could lay hands on. I squirmed about on my belly for a long time, and in the end I managed to get up. But still I couldn't reckon out where I was, nor what had happened to me. My memory was clean gone. But I was scared to lie down. I was scared I'd never get up again, so I just stood there swaying from side to side like a poplar in a gale.

"When I came to myself and had a look round, my heart felt as if someone had got a pair of pliers round it. The shells I'd been carrying were lying about all round me, not far away was my lorry, all torn to bits, with its wheels in the air, and the fighting, the fighting was going on behind me.... Yes, behind me!

"When I realized that, and I'm not ashamed to say it, my legs just caved in under me and I fell as if I'd been pole-axed, because I realized I was cut off behind the enemy lines, or to put it point-blank, I was already a prisoner of the fascists. That's war for you....

"No, it's not an easy thing to understand, mate, it's not easy to understand that you've got taken prisoner through no wish of your own. And it takes time to explain to a fellow who's never felt it on his own hide, just what that thing means.

"So I lay there and soon I heard the tanks rumbling. Four medium German tanks went by me at full speed in the direction I'd brought the shells from. What do you think that felt like? Then came the tractors hauling the guns, and a mobile kitchen, then the infantry, not many of 'em, not more than a company all told. I'd squint up at them out of the corner of my eye and then I'd press my face into the earth again; it made me sick to look at them, sick in my soul....

"When I thought they'd all gone past, I lifted my head, and there were six submachine-gunners marching along about a hundred paces away. And as I looked they turned off the road and came straight towards me, all six of 'em, without saying a word. Well, I thought, this is it. So I got into a sitting position—I didn't want to die lying down—and then I stood up. One of them stopped a few paces away from me and jerked his gun off his shoulder. And it's funny how a man's made, but at that moment I didn't feel any panic, not even a shiver in my heart. I just looked at him and thought: 'It's going to be a short burst, I wonder where he'll place it?

At my head or across my chest?' As if it mattered a damn to me what part of my body he made his holes in.

"Young fellow he was, pretty well built, dark-haired, but his lips were thin as thread, and his eyes had a nasty glint in them. That one won't think twice about shooting me down, I thought. And sure enough, up goes his gun. I looked him straight in the eye and didn't say anything. But another one, a corporal or something, older than him, almost elderly to look at, shouted something, then pushed the other fellow aside and came up to me. He babbled something in his own language and bent my right elbow, feeling my muscle he was. 'O-o-oh!' he says when he feels it, and pointed along the road to where the sun was setting, as much as to say: 'Off you go, you mule, and work for our Reich.' Thrifty type he was, the son-of-a-bitch!

"But the dark-haired one had got his eye on my boots and they looked a good sound pair, so he signs with his hand: 'Take 'em off!' I sat down on the ground, took off my boots and handed them to him. Fair snatched them out of my hands he did. So I unwound my footcloths and held them out to him, looking up at him from the ground. But he shouted and swore, and up went his gun again. And the others just roared with laughter. And so they went away. Only the dark-haired one, he looked round at me about three times before he got to the road, and his eyes glittered like a wolf-cub's with fury. Anyone would think I'd taken his boots instead of him taking mine.

"Well, mate, there was nothing for it. I went on to the road, let out the longest and hottest Voronezh cuss I could think of, and stepped out westward—a prisoner! But I wasn't much good for walking by that time, a kilometre an hour was all I could do, not more. It was like being drunk. You'd try to go straight and something would just push you from one side of the road to the other. I went on for a bit and then a column of our prisoners from the same division as I'd been in caught up with me. There were about ten German submachine-gunners guarding them. The one at the front of the column came up to me and, without saying a word, just bashed me on the head with his gun. If I'd gone down, he'd have stitched me to the ground with a burst, but our chaps caught me as I fell and hustled me into the middle of the column and half carried me along for a while. And when I came to, one of them whispered: 'Don't fall down for God's sake! Keep going while you've got any strength left, or they'll kill you!' And though I had mighty little strength left, I managed to keep going.

"As soon as the sun went down the Germans strengthened their guard, brought up another twenty submachine-gunners in a lorry, and drove us on at a quicker pace. The badly wounded ones couldn't keep up with the rest, and they shot them down in the road. Two tried to make a break for it, but they forgot that on a moonlit night you can be seen a mile away out in the open; of course, they got shot too. At midnight we came to a village that was half burned down. They drove us into a church with a smashed dome. We spent the night on the stone floor without a scrap of straw, and no one had a greatcoat, we were all in our tunics, so there wasn't anything to lie on. Some of us didn't even have tunics, just calico undershirts. They were mostly NCOs. They had taken off their tunics so they couldn't be told from the rank and file. And the men from the gun crews hadn't got tunics either. They had been taken prisoner half-naked as they were while working at the guns.

"That night it poured with rain and we all got wet to the skin. Part of the roof had been smashed by a heavy shell or a bomb and the rest of it was ripped up by shrapnel; there wasn't a dry spot even at the altar. And so we spent the whole night in that church, like sheep in a dark pen. In the middle of the night I felt someone touch my arm and ask: 'Are you wounded, comrade?' 'Why do you ask, mate?' I says. 'I'm a doctor, perhaps I can help you in some way.' I told him my left shoulder made a creaking noise and was swollen and gave me terrible pain. And he says firmly: 'Take off your tunic and undershirt.' I took everything off and he started feeling about with his thin fingers round my shoulder, and did it hurt! I ground my teeth and I says to him: 'You must be a vet, not a doctor. Why do you press just where it hurts, you heartless devil?' But he kept on groping about, and he says to me, angry like: 'Your job's to keep your mouth shut! Talking to me like that! Just wait, it'll hurt more in a minute.' And then he gave my arm such a wrench that red sparks spurted out of my eyes.

"When I got my senses back I asked him: 'What are you doing, you fascist bastard. My arm's broken to bits and you give it a pull like that.' I heard him chuckle, then he said: 'I thought you'd hit out with your right while I was doing it, but you're a good-tempered chap, it seems. Your arm wasn't broken, it was out of joint and I've put it back in its socket. Well, feeling any better?' And sure enough, I could feel the pain going out of me. I thanked him from the bottom of my heart and he went on in the darkness, asking quietly: 'Any wounded?' There was a real doctor for you. Even shut up like that, in pitch darkness, he went on doing his great work.

"It was a restless night. They wouldn't let us out even to relieve ourselves, the senior guard had told us that when he drove us into the church in pairs. And as luck would have it, one of the Christians among us wanted to go out bad. He kept on saving it up and at last he burst into tears. 'I can't pollute a holy place!' he says. 'I'm a believer, I'm a Christian. What shall I do, lads?' And you know the kind of chaps we were. Some laughed, others cursed, and others started teasing him with all sorts of advice. Cheered us all up, he did, but it turned out bad in the end. He started bashing on the door and asking to be let out. And he got his answer. A fascist gave a long burst through the door with his submachine-gun, killed the Christian and three more with him, and another was so badly wounded he died by morning.

"We pulled the dead into a corner, then sat down quiet and thought to ourselves, this isn't a very cheerful start. And presently we started whispering to each other, asking each other where we came from and how we'd got taken prisoner. The chaps who'd been in the same platoon or the same company started calling quietly to each other in the darkness. And next to me I heard two voices talking. One of them says: 'Tomorrow, if they form us up before they take us on farther and call out for the commissars, Communists, and Jews, you needn't try and hide yourself, platoon commander. You won't get away with it. You think just because you've taken off your tunic you'il pass for a ranker? Well, that won't wash! I'm not going to suffer because of you. I'll be the first to point you out. I know you're a Communist. I remember how you tried to get me to join the Party, now you're going to answer for it.' That was the one sitting nearest to me, on the left, and on the other side of him, a young voice answers: 'I always suspected you were a rotten type, Kryzhnev. Specially when you refused to join the Party, pretending you were illiterate. But I never thought you'd turn out to be a traitor. You went to school until you were fourteen, didn't you?' And the other one answers in a lazy sort of way: 'Yes, I did. So what?' They were quiet for a long time, and the platoon commander—I could tell him by his voice—says softly: 'Don't give me away, Comrade Kryzhnev.' And the other one laughed quietly. 'You've left your comrades behind on the other side of the line,' he says, 'I'm no comrade of yours, so don't plead with me, I'm going to point you out all the same. I believe in looking after my own skin first.'

"They stopped talking and my whole body shuddered at the thought of such a creeping low-down action. 'No,' I thought, 'I won't let you betray your commander, you son-of-a-bitch. You won't walk out of this church on your own two feet, they'll drag you out by the legs!' Then it began to get light and I could see a fellow with a big fleshy face lying on his back with his hands behind his head, and beside him a little snub-nosed lad, in only an under-shirt, sitting with his arms round his knees and looking very pale. 'That kid won't be able to handle this great fat gelding,' I thought. 'I'll have to finish him off myself.'

"I touched the lad's arm and asked him in a whisper: 'You a platoon commander?' He didn't say anything, just nodded. 'That one over there wants to give you away?' I pointed to the fellow lying on his back. He nodded again. 'All right,' I said, 'hold his legs so he won't kick! And quick about it!' And I jumped on that fellow and locked my fingers round his throat. He didn't even have time to shout. I held him under me for a few minutes, then eased off a bit. That was one traitor less, with his tongue hanging out!

"It was a rotten feeling I had after that, and I wanted to wash my hands something terrible, as if it wasn't a man I'd killed but some crawling snake.... The first time I had killed anyone in my life, and one of our own. Our own? But he wasn't anything of the kind. He was worse than one of the enemy, he was a traitor. I got up and said to the platoon commander: 'Let's go away from here, comrade, the church is a big place.'

"Just as that Kryzhnev had said, in the morning we were all formed up outside the church with a ring of submachine-gunners covering us, and three SS officers started picking out the ones among us they thought were dangerous. They asked who were Communists, who were officers, who were commissars, but they didn't find any. And they didn't find anybody who was swine enough to give them away either, because nearly half of us were Communists, and there were a lot of officers, too, and commissars. They only took four out of over two hundred men. One Jew and three Russians from the rank and file. The Russians landed in trouble because they were all dark and had curly hair. The SS men just came up to them and said: '*Jude?*' The one they asked would say he was a Russian, but they wouldn't even listen. 'Step out!' and that was that.

"They shot the poor devils and drove us on further. The platoon commander who'd helped me strangle that traitor kept by me right as far as Poznan, and the first day of the march he'd edge up to me every now and then and press my hand as we went along. At Poznan we got separated. It happened like this.

"You see, mate, ever since the day I was captured I'd been thinking of escaping. But I wanted to make sure of it. All the way to Poznan, where they put us in a proper camp, I never got the right kind of chance. But in the Poznan camp it looked as if I'd got what I wanted. At the end of May they sent us out to a little wood near the camp to dig graves for the prisoners that had died, a lot of our chaps died at that time from dysentery, and while I was digging away at that Poznan clay I had a look round and I noticed that two of our guards had sat down to have a bite, and the third one was dozing in the sun. I put down my shovel and went off quietly behind a bush. And then I ran for it, keeping straight towards the sunrise.

"They couldn't have noticed me very quick, those guards. Where I found the strength, skinny as I was, to cover nearly forty kilometres in one day, I don't know myself. But nothing came of it. On the fourth day, when I was a long way from that cursed camp, they caught me. There were bloodhounds on my track, and they found me in a field of unreaped oats.

"At dawn I came to an open field and I was afraid to go across it in the daylight and it was at least three kilometres to the woods, so I lay low in the oats for the day. I crushed up some oat grains in my hand and was filling my pockets with a supply, when I heard the sound of dogs barking and the roar of a motorcycle. My heart missed a beat because the dogs kept coming nearer. I lay flat and covered my head with my arms, so they wouldn't bite my face. Well, they came up and it only took them a minute to tear all my rags off me.

I was left in nothing but what I was born in. They dragged me about in the oats, just did what they liked with me, and in the end a big dog got his forepaws on my chest and started making passes at my throat, but he didn't bite straight way.

"Two Germans came up on motor-cycles. First they beat me up good and proper, then they set the dogs on me, and the flesh just came off me in chunks. They took me back to camp, naked and bloody as I was. I got a month in solitary for trying to escape, but I was still alive.... I managed to keep alive somehow!

"It's pretty awful, mate, to remember the things I went through as a prisoner, let alone tell you about them. When you remember the inhuman tortures we had to suffer out there, in Germany, when you remember all your mates who were tortured to death in those camps, your heart comes up and starts beating in your throat and it's hard to breathe.

"The way they herded us about in those two years I was a prisoner! I reckon I covered half of Germany being driven from camp to camp. I was in Saxony, at a silicate plant, in the Ruhr, hauling coal in a mine. I sweated away with a shovel in Bavaria, I had a spell in Thüringen, and the devil knows what German soil I didn't have to tread. There's plenty of different scenery out there, but the way they shot and bashed our lads was the same all over. And those God-damned reptiles and parasites lammed into us like no man here ever beat an animal. Punching us, kicking us, beating us with rubber truncheons, with any lump of iron they happened to have handy, not to mention their rifle butts and sticks.

"They beat you up just because you were a Russian, because you were still alive in the world, just because you worked for them. And they'd beat you for giving them a wrong look, taking a wrong step, for not turning round the way they wanted.... They beat you just so that one day they'd knock the life out of you, so you'd choke with your own blood and die of beating. There weren't enough ovens in the whole of Germany, I reckon, for all of us to be shoved into.

"And everywhere we went they fed us the same: hundred and fifty grams of ersatz bread made half of sawdust, and a thin swill of swedes. Some places they gave us hot water to drink, some places they didn't. But what's the use of talking, judge for yourself. Before the war started I weighed eighty-six kilograms, and by the autumn I couldn't turn more than fifty. Just skin and bones, and hardly enough strength to carry the bones either. But you had to work, and not say a word, and the work we did would have been a lot too much for a cart-horse sometimes, I reckon.

"At the beginning of September they sent a hundred and forty-two of us Soviet prisoners-of-war from a camp near Küstrin to camp B-14, not far from Dresden. At that time there were about two thousand in that camp. We were all working in a stone quarry, cutting and crushing their German stone by hand. The stint was four cubic metres a day per man, and for a man, mind you, who could hardly keep body and soul together anyway. And then it really started. After two months, out of the hundred and forty-two men in our group there were only fifty-seven left. How about that, mate? Tough going, eh? We hardly had time to bury our own mates, and then there was a rumour in the camp that the Germans had taken Stalingrad and were pressing on into Siberia. It was one grief after another, and they held us down so we couldn't lift our eyes from the ground, as if we were just asking to be put there, into that German earth. And every day the camp guard were drinking and bawling out their songs, rejoicing for all they were worth.

"One evening we came back to our hut from work. It had been raining all day and our rags were soaking; we were all shivering from the cold wind and couldn't stop our teeth chattering. There wasn't anywhere to get dry or warm, and we were as hungry as death itself, or even worse. But we were never given any food in the evenings.

"Well, I took off my wet rags, threw them on to my bunk and said: 'They want you to do four cubic metres a day, but one cubic metre would be plenty to bury one of us.' That was all I said, but, would you believe it, among our own fellows there was one dirty dog who went and reported my bitter words to the camp commandant.

"The camp commandant, or *Lagerführer*, as they call him, was a German called Müller. Not very tall, thick-set, hair like a bunch of tow; sort of bleached all over. The hair on his head, his eyelashes, even his eyes were a kind of faded colour, and he was pop-eyed too. Spoke Russian like you and me, even had a bit of a Volga accent, as if he'd been born and bred in those parts. And could he swear! He was a terror for it. I sometimes wonder where the bastard ever learned that trade. He'd form us up in front of the block—that's what they

called the hut—and walk down the line sur-
rounded by his bunch of SS men with his right
hand held back. He wore a leather glove and
under the leather there was a strip of lead to
protect his fingers. He'd walk down the line
and bloody every other man's nose for him.
'Inoculation against flu,' he used to call it. And
so it went on every day. Altogether there were
four blocks in the camp, and one day he'd give
the first block their 'inoculation,' next day, the
second, and so on. Regular bastard he was,
never took a day off. There was only one thing
he didn't understand, the fool; before he started on his round, he'd stand out in front there,
and to get himself real worked up for it, he'd
start cursing. He'd stand there cursing away
for all he was worth, and, do you know, he'd
make us feel a bit better. You see, the words
sounded like our own, it was like a breath of
air from over there. If he'd known his cursing
and swearing gave us pleasure, I reckon he
wouldn't have done it in Russian, he'd have
stuck to his own language. Only one of our
fellows, a pal of mine from Moscow, used to
get wild with him. 'When he curses like that,'
he says, 'I shut my eyes and think I'm in
Moscow, having one at the local, and it just
makes me dizzy for a glass of beer.'

"Well, the day after I said that about the cubic metres, that commandant had me up on the mat. In the evening an interpreter and two guards came to our hut. 'Sokolov Andrei?' I answered. 'Follow us, quick march, the *Herr Lagerführer* himself wants to see you.' I guessed what he wanted me for. To finish me off. So I said good-bye to my pals, they all knew I was going to my death, took a deep breath and followed the guards. I went across the camp yard, looked up at the stars and said good-bye to them, and I thought to myself: Well, you've had your full dose of torture, Andrei Sokolov, Number 331. I felt somehow sorry for Irina and the kids, then I got over it and began screwing up my courage to face the barrel of that pistol without flinching, like a soldier should, so the enemy wouldn't see how hard it'd be for me at the last minute to part with this life. . . .

"In the commandant's room there were flowers on the window-sill and it was clean and nice as it is in one of our clubs. At the table there were all the camp's officers. Five of 'em, sitting there, downing schnapps and chewing bacon fat. On the table there was a big opened bottle, bread, bacon fat, soused apples, all kinds of open tins. I took one glance at all that grub, and you wouldn't believe it, but I felt so sick I nearly vomited. I was hungry as a wolf, you see, and I'd forgotten what the sight of human food was like, and now there was all this stuff in front of me. Somehow I kept my sickness down, but it cost me a great effort to tear my eyes away from that table.

"Right in front of me sat Müller, half-drunk, flicking his pistol from one hand to the other, playing with it, and he'd got his eye fixed on me, like a snake. Well, I stood to attention, snapped my broken-down heels together, and reported in a loud voice like this: 'Prisoner-of-war Andrei Sokolov at your service. *Herr Kommandant.*' And he says to me: 'Well, you Russian Ivan, four cubic metres of quarrying is too much for you, is it?' 'Yes, *Herr Kommandant*,' I said, 'it is.' 'And is one cubic metre enough to make a grave for you?' 'Yes, *Herr Kommandant*, quite enough and to spare.'

"He gets up and says: 'I shall do you a great honour, I shall now shoot you in person for those words. It will make a mess here, so come into the yard, you can sign off out there.' 'As you like,' I told him. He stood thinking for a minute, then tossed his pistol on the table and poured out a full glass of schnapps, took a piece of bread, put a slice of fat on it, held the lot out to me and says: 'Before you die, Russian Ivan, drink to the triumph of German arms.'

"I was about to take the glass and the bread out of his hand, but when I heard those words, something seemed to burn me inside. Me, a Russian soldier, I thought, drink to the victory of German arms?! What'll you want next, *Herr Kommandant?* You can go to hell with your schnapps!

"I put the glass down on the table, and the bread with it, and I said: 'Thank you for your hospitality, but I don't drink.' He smiles. 'So you don't want to drink to our victory? In that case, drink to your own death.' What had I got to lose? 'To my death and relief from torment then,' I said. And with that, I took the glass and poured it down my throat in two gulps. But I didn't touch the bread. I just wiped my lips politely with my hand and said: 'Thank you for your hospitality. I am ready, *Herr Kommandant,* you can sign me off now.'

"But he was looking at me sharply and he says: 'Have a bite to eat before you die.' So I says to him: 'I never eat after the first glass.' Then he poured out a second and handed it to me. I drank the second and again I didn't touch the food, I was staking everything on courage, you see. Anyway, I thought, I'll get drunk before I go out into that yard to die. And the commandant's fair eyebrows shot up in the air. 'Why don't you eat, Russian Ivan? Don't be shy!' But I stuck to my guns: 'Excuse me, *Herr Kommandant*, but I don't eat after the second glass either.' He puffed up his cheeks and snorted, and then he gave such a roar of laughter, and while he laughed he said something quickly in German, must have been translating my words to his friends. The others laughed too, pushed their chairs back, turned their big mugs round to look at me, and I noticed something different in their looks, something a bit softer like.

"The commandant poured me out a third glass and his hands were shaking with laughter. I drank that glass slowly, bit off a little bit of bread and put the rest down on the table. I wanted to show the bastards that even though I was half dead with hunger I wasn t going to choke myself with the scraps they flung me, that I had my own, Russian dignity and pride, and that they hadn't turned me into an animal as they had wanted to.

"After that the commandant got a serious look on his face, straightened the two iron crosses on his chest, came out from behind the table unarmed and said: 'Look here, Sokolov, you're a real Russian soldier. You're a fine soldier. I am a soldier, too, and I respect a worthy enemy. I shall not shoot you. What is more, today our gallant armies have reached the Volga and taken complete possession of Stalingrad. That is a great joy for us, and therefore I graciously grant you your life. Go to your block and take this with you for your courage.' And he handed me a smallish loaf of bread from the table, and a lump of bacon fat.

"I gripped that bread to my chest tight as I could, and picked up the fat in my left hand, and I was so taken aback at this unexpected turn of events that I didn't even say thank you, just did a left-about turn, and went to the door. And all the while I was thinking, now he'll blast daylight through my shoulder blades and I'll never get this grub back to the lads. But no, nothing happened. Again death passed me by and I only felt the cold breath of it.

"I got out of the commandant's room without a stagger, but outside I went reeling all over the place. I lurched into the hut and pitched flat down on the cement floor, unconscious. The lads woke me up when it was still dark: 'Tell us what happened!' Then I remembered what had happened at the commandant's and told them. 'How are we going to share out the grub?' the man in the bunk next to me asked, and his voice was trembling. 'Equal shares all round,' I told him. We waited till it got light. We cut up the bread and fat with a bit of thread. Each of us got a lump of bread about the size of a match-box, not a crumb was wasted, and as for the fat, well, of course, there was only enough to grease your lips with. But we shared it out fair for all.

"Soon they put about three hundred of the strongest of us on draining a marsh, then off we went to the Ruhr to work in the mines. And there I stayed until 'forty-four. By that time our lads had knocked some of the stuffing out of Germany and the fascists had stopped looking down on us, prisoners. One day they lined us up, the whole day shift, and some visiting *Oberleutnant* said through an interpreter: 'Anyone who served in the army or worked before the war as a driver, one pace forward.' About seven of us who'd been drivers before stepped out. They gave us some old overalls and took us under guard to Potsdam. When we got there, we were split up. I was detailed to work in Todt. That was what the Germans called the set-up they had for building roads and defence works.

"I drove a German major of the engineers about in an Opel-Admiral. That was a fascist hog for you if you like! Short fellow with a pot belly, as broad as he was tall, and a back-side on him as big as any wench's. He had three chins hanging down over his collar in front, and three whopping folds round his neck at the back. Must have carried a good hundred-weight of pure fat on him, I should think. When he walked, he puffed like a steam-engine, and when he sat down to eat—hold tight! He'd go on all day, chewing and taking swigs from his flask of brandy. Now and then I came in for a bit too. He'd stop on the road, cut up some sausage and cheese, and have a drink; and when he was in a good mood he'd toss me a scrap like a dog. Never handed it to me, oh, no, he considered that beneath him. But be that as it may, there was no comparing it to the camp, and little by little I began to look like a man again, I even began to put on weight.

"For about two weeks I drove the major to and fro between Potsdam and Berlin, then he was sent to the front-line area to build de-fences against our troops. And then I just forgot how to sleep at night. All night long I'd be thinking how to escape to my own fellows, my own country.

"We drove to the town of Polotsk. At dawn, for the first time in two years I heard the boom of our artillery, and you can guess how my heart thumped at the sound. Why, mate, even when I first started courting Irina, it never beat like that! The fighting was going on east of Polotsk, about eighteen kilometres away. The Germans in the town were sore as hell, and jumpy, and my old pot-belly started drinking more and more. During the daytime he would drive round and he'd give instructions on how to build the fortifications, and at night he'd sit by himself drinking. He got all puffy, and there were great bags under his eyes.

"Well, I thought, no need to wait any longer, this is my chance. And I'm not just going to escape alone, I've got to take old pot-belly with me, he'll come in useful over there!

"Among some ruins I found a heavy iron weight and wound a rag round it, so that if I had to hit him there wouldn't be any blood, picked up a length of telephone wire in the road, got everything ready that I needed, and hid it all under the front seat. One evening, two days before I said good-bye to the Germans, I was on my way back from the filling station and I saw a German *Unter* staggering along blind drunk, grabbing at the wall. I

47

pulled up, led him into a damaged building and shook him out of his uniform, and took his cap off his head. Then I hid the whole lot under the seat and I was ready.

"On the morning of June 29th, my major told me to take him out of town in the direction of Trosnitsa. He was in charge of some defence works that were being built there. We drove off. The major was sitting on the back seat taking a quiet doze, and I sat in front with my heart trying to jump out of my mouth. I drove fast, but outside the town I slowed down, then stopped and got out and had a look round; a long way behind there were two lorries coming on slowly. I got out my iron weight and opened the door wide. Old pot-belly was lying back on the seat, snoring as if he'd got his wife beside him. Well, I gave him a bang on the left temple with my iron. His head flopped on to his chest. Just to make sure, I gave him another one, but I didn't want to kill him. I wanted to take him over alive, he was going to be able to tell our lads a lot of things. So I pulled the parabellum out of his holster and shoved it in my pocket. Then I pushed a bracket down behind the back seat, tied the telephone wire round the major's neck and fastened it to the bracket. That was so he wouldn't tumble over on his side when I drove fast. I pulled on the German uniform and cap, and drove the car straight for the place where the earth was rumbling, where the fighting was.

"I ripped across the German front line between two pill-boxes. A bunch of subma- chine-gunners popped up out of a dug-out and I slowed down purposely so they would see I had a major with me. They started shouting and waving their arms to show me I mustn't go on, but I pretended not to understand and roared off at about eighty. Before they realized what was happening and opened fire I was on no man's land, weaving round the shell- holes no worse than any hare.

"There were the Germans firing from be- hind, and then our own chaps got fierce and had a smack at me from the front. Put four bullets through the wind-screen, shot up the radiator. But not far away I spotted a little wood near a lake, and some of our chaps running to- wards the car, so I drove into the wood, flung the door open, fell on the ground and kissed it. And I could hardly breathe.

"A young fellow, with a kind of khaki shoul- der-straps on his tunic I'd never seen before, reached me first and says with a grin: 'Aha, you Fritzy devil, lost your way, eh?' I tore off my German tunic, threw the German cap down at my feet, and I says to him: 'You lovely young kid. Sonny boy! Me a Fritz when I was born and bred in Voronezh! I was a prisoner-of-war, see? And now unhitch that fat hog sitting in the car, take his brief-case and lead him off to your commander.' I handed over my pistol and was passed from one person to the next until by the evening I had to report to the colonel in command of the division. By that time I had been fed and taken to the bath-house and questioned, and given a new uni-form, so I went to the colonel's dug-out in proper order, clean in body and soul, and properly dressed. The colonel got up from his table, and came up to me, and in front of all the officers there, he takes me in his arms and says: 'Thank you, soldier, for the fine gift you brought us. Your major and his brief-case have told us more than any twenty Germans we might capture on the front line. I shall rec-ommend you for a decoration.' His words and the affection he showed moved me so much I couldn't keep my lips from trembling, and all I could say was: 'Comrade Colonel, I request to be enrolled in an infantry unit.'

"But the colonel laughed and clapped me on the shoulder. 'What kind of a fighter do you think you'd make when you can hardly stand on your feet? I'm sending you off to hospital straightaway. They'll patch you up there and put some food inside you, and after that you'll go home to your family for a month's leave, and when you come back to us, we'll think out where to put you.'

"The colonel and all the officers that were in the dug-out with him, shook hands and said good-bye to me in a heart-felt way, and I went out with my head spinning because in the two years I'd been away I'd forgotten what it was like to be treated like a human being. And mind you, mate, it was a long time before I got out of the habit of ducking my head into my shoulders when I had to talk to the high-ups, as if I was still scared of being hit. That was the kind of training we got in those fascist camps....

"As soon as I got into hospital I wrote Irina a letter. I told her in a few words all about how I was taken prisoner and how I escaped with the German major. Where that kid's boasting came from in me, I couldn't tell you. Why, I couldn't even hold back from saying the colonel had promised to recommend me for a medal....

"For a couple of weeks I just slept and ate.

4*   51

They fed me up a little at a time, but often; if they'd given me all the food I wanted, so the doctor said, I might have gone under. But after two weeks was up, I couldn't look at food. There was no reply from home and, I must admit, I began to get mopy. Couldn't think of eating, sleep wouldn't come to me, and all kinds of bad thoughts kept creeping into my head. In the third week I got a letter from Voronezh. But it wasn't from Irina, it was from a neighbour of mine, a joiner. I wouldn't wish anyone to get a letter like that. He wrote that the Germans had bombed the aircraft factory, and one heavy bomb had fallen plumb on my cottage. Irina and the girls were at home when it dropped. . . . Well, he wrote that they didn't find a trace of them, and there was only a deep crater where the house had been. . . . First time I didn't manage to finish reading that letter. Everything went dark before my eyes and my heart squeezed into a tight little ball so that I thought it would never open up again. I lay back on my bed and got a bit of strength back, then I read to the end. My neighbour wrote that Anatoly had been in town during the bombing. In the evening he went to the spot where his home had been, looked at the bomb-crater and went back to town the same night.

Before he went, he told my neighbour he was going to volunteer for the front. And that was all.

"When my heart eased up and I heard the blood rushing in my ears, I remembered how Irina had clung to me when we parted at the station. That woman's heart of hers must have known all along we were not to see each other again in this world. And I had pushed her away.... Once I had had a family, a home of my own, it had all taken years to build, and it was all destroyed in a flash, and I was left all alone. It must be a dream, I thought, this messed-up life of mine. Why, when I had been a prisoner, nearly every night, under my breath, of course, I had talked to Irina and the kids, tried to cheer them up by telling them I'd come home and they needn't grieve; I'm tough, I said, I can stand it, we'll all be together again one day. So for two years I had been talking to the dead?!..."

The big man was silent for a minute, then he said jerkily in a changed, quiet tone: "Let's have a smoke, mate, I feel somehow as if I was choking."

We lighted up. A woodpecker tapped resonantly in the flooded woodland. The warm breeze still rustled the dry leaves of the alders, the clouds were still floating past in the towering blue, as though under taut white sails, but in those minutes of solemn silence the boundless world preparing for the great fulfilment of spring, for that eternal affirmation of the living in life, seemed quite different to me.

It was too distressing to keep silent and I asked:

"What happened then?"

"What happened then?" the story-teller responded unwillingly. "Then I got a month's leave from the colonel, and a week later I was in Voronezh. I went on foot to the place where I had once lived with my family. There was a deep crater full of rusty water, the weeds all round came up to your waist. Everywhere empty and still, still as a graveyard. I felt it bad then, mate, I can tell you! I stood there and let my soul grieve, then I went back to the station. I couldn't stay there an hour, and the same day I went back to the division.

"But about three months later I did get a flash of joy, like a gleam of sunlight through the clouds. I got news of Anatoly. He sent me a letter from another front. He had got to know my address from that neighbour of mine. It seems he'd been to an artillery college to start with; his gift for mathematics stood him in good stead there. After a year he passed out with honours and went to the front, and now he wrote he had been given the rank of captain, was commanding a battery of 'forty-fives,' and had been awarded six Orders and medals. In a word, he'd left his old man far behind. And again I felt real proud of him. Say what you like, but my own son was a captain and commander of a battery, that was something! And all those decorations too. It didn't matter that his dad was just carting shells and other stuff about in a Studebaker. His dad's time was past, but he, a captain, had everything ahead of him.

"And at nights I began having old man's dreams. When the war was over I'd get my son married and live with them. I'd do a bit of carpentry and look after the kiddies. All the kind of things an old man does. But that all went bust too. In the winter we went on advancing without a break and there wasn't time to write to each other very often, but towards the end of the war, right up near Berlin, I sent Anatoly a letter one morning and got an answer the very next day. It turned out that he and I had come up to the German capital by different routes and were now very close to each other. I could hardly wait for the moment when we'd meet. Well, the moment came.... Right on the ninth of May, on the morning of Victory Day, my Anatoly was killed by a German sniper.

"In the afternoon I was called up before a company commander. I saw there was a strange artillery officer sitting with him. I went into the room and he stood up as if he was meeting a senior. My company commander said: 'He's come to see you, Sokolov,' and turned away to the window. Something went through me then like an electric shock, because I felt trouble coming. The lieutenant-colonel came up to me and said: 'Bear up, father. Your son, Captain Sokolov, was killed today at his battery. Come with me.'

"I swayed, but I kept my feet. Even now it seems like a dream the way that lieutenant-colonel and I drove in that big car along those streets strewn with rubble. I've only a foggy memory of the soldiers drawn up in line and the coffin covered with red velvet. But my Anatoly I see as plain as I can see you now, mate. I went up to the coffin. Yes, it was my son lying there, and yet it wasn't. My son had been a lad, always smiling, with narrow shoulders and a sharp little Adam's apple sticking out of his thin neck, but here was a young broad-shouldered handsome full-grown man, his eyes were half-closed as if he was looking past me into some far unknown distance. Only the corners of his lips still had a bit of the smile my son used to have. The Anatoly I knew once. I kissed him and stepped aside. The lieutenant-colonel made a speech. My Anatoly's friends were wiping their tears, but I couldn't cry, I reckon the tears dried up in my heart. Mebbe that's why it still hurts so much.

"I buried my last joy and hope in that foreign German soil, the battery fired a volley to send off their commander on his long journey, and something seemed to snap inside me.... When I got back to my unit I was not myself. Soon after that I was demobilized. Where was I to go? To Voronezh? Not for anything! I remembered I had a friend who had been invalided out of the army back in the winter and was living in Uryupinsk; he had asked me to go and live with him once. so I went.

"My friend and his wife had no children and they had their own cottage on the edge of the town. He got a disability pension, but he worked as a driver in a lorry depot and I got a job there too. I settled with my friend and they gave me a home. We used to drive various loads about the suburbs and in the autumn we switched over to grain delivery work. It was then I got to know my new son, the one that's playing down there in the sand.

"First thing you'd do when you got back from a long trip would be to go to a caf' for a bite of something, and of course, you'd put away a glass of vodka to get rid of your tiredness. I had quite a liking for that harmful habit by that time, I must admit. And one day I noticed this lad near the caf', and the next day I noticed him again. What a little ragamuffin he was! His face all smeared with watermelon juice and dust, dirty as anything, hair all over the place, but he'd got a pair of eyes like stars at night after it's been raining! And I felt so fond of him that, funny though it may seem, I started missing him, and I'd hurry to finish my run so I could get back to the caf' and see him sooner. That's where he got his food—he ate what people gave him.

"The fourth day I came in straight from the state farm with my lorry loaded with grain and pulled in at the caf'. There was my little fellow sitting on the steps, kicking his legs, and pretty hungry by the look of him. I poked my head out of the window and shouted to him: 'Hi, Vanya! Come on, jump aboard, I'll take you to the elevator, and then we'll come back here and have some dinner.' My shout made him start, then he jumped straight from the steps on to the running board and pulled himself up to the window. 'How do you know my name's Vanya?' he says quietly, and he opens those starry eyes of his wide, waiting for my answer. Well, I told him I was just one of those chaps who know everything.

"He came round to the right side, I opened the door and let him in beside me, and off we went. Lively little fellow he was, but suddenly he got quiet, and from time to time gave me a look from under those long curly eyelashes of his, and sighed. Such a little fellow and he'd already learned to sigh. Was that the thing for him to be doing? 'Where's your father, Vanya?' I asked. 'He was killed at the front,' he whispered. 'And Mummy?' 'Mummy was killed by a bomb when we were in the train.' 'Where were you coming from in the train?' 'I don't know, I don't remember....' 'And haven't you got any family at all?' 'No, nobody.' 'But where do you sleep at night?' 'Anywhere I can find.'

"I felt the hot tears welling up in my throat and I made up my mind at once. Why should we suffer alone and separate like this! I'd take him in as my own son. And straightaway I felt easier in my mind and there was a sort of brightness there. I leaned over to him and asked very quiet like: 'Vanya, do you know who I am?' And he just breathed it out: 'Who?' And still as quiet, I says to him: 'I'm your father.'

"Lord alive, what happened then! He threw his arms round my neck, he kissed my cheeks, my lips, my forehead, and started chirping away like a singing bird: 'Daddy dear! I knew it! I knew you'd find me! I knew you'd find me whatever happened! I've been waiting so long for you to find me!' He pressed himself to me and he was trembling all over, like a blade of grass in the wind. My eyes were misty, and I was trembling too, and my hands were shaking.... How I managed to keep hold of the wheel I don't know. Even so I put her in the ditch and stopped the engine. While my eyes were so misty I was afraid to go in case I knocked someone down. We sat there for about five minutes and my little son was still clinging to me for all he was worth, and not saying anything, just trembling. I put my right arm round him, hugged him gently, and turned the lorry round with my left hand and drove back to the cottage where I lived. I couldn't think about going to the elevator after that.

"I left the lorry at the gate, took my new son

in my arms and carried him into the house.
And he got his little arms round my neck and
hung on tight. He pressed his cheek to my
unshaven chin and stuck there. And that's how
I carried him in. My friend and his wife were
both at home. I came in and winked at them
with both eyes, and bold and cheerful I says:
'Well, I've found my little Vanya at last. Here
we are, good people.' They hadn't got any
children themselves and they both wanted a
kid, so they guessed what was up straightaway
and started bustling around. And I just
couldn't get away from my son. But somehow I
managed to persuade him. I washed his hands
with soap, sat him down at the table. My
friend's wife ladled him out a plate of soup,
and when she saw how he gulped it down, she
just burst into tears. She stood at the stove,
crying into her apron. And my Vanya, he saw
she was crying, and he ran up to her, tugged
at her skirt and said: 'Why are you crying,
Auntie? Daddy found me near the café. Every-
body ought to be happy. and you are crying.'
But she only cried all the harder, made herself
all wet, she did!

"After dinner I took him to the barber's and
had his hair cut, and at home I gave him a
bath myself in a tub and wrapped him up in a

clean sheet. He put his arms round me and went to sleep in my arms. I laid him gently in bed, drove off to the elevator, unloaded the grain, took the lorry back to the park and ran off to the shops. I bought him a pair of serge trousers, a little shirt, a pair of sandals and a straw cap. Of course, it all turned out to be the wrong size and no good for quality. My friend's wife even gave me a ticking-off over the trousers. 'Are you crazy,' she says, 'dressing a boy in serge trousers in heat like this!' And the next minute she had the sewing machine on the table and was rummaging in the chest, and in an hour she had a pair of cotton trousers and a little white shirt ready for my Vanya. I took him to bed with me and for the first time for many a night fell asleep peacefully. I woke up about four times in the night though. And there he was, nestling in the crook of my arm, like a sparrow under the eaves, breathing away softly, and I can't find words to tell you how much joy I felt. I'd try not to move so as not to disturb him, but it was no good. I'd get up very quiet, light a match and just stand there, admiring him. . . .

"Just before daybreak I woke up and I couldn't make out why it seemed so stuffy. And it was my little son, he'd climbed out of his sheet and was lying right across my chest, with his little foot on my throat. He's a rare young fidget to sleep with, he is, but I've got used to him, I miss him when he's not there. At night, you can look at him while he's sleeping, or you can smell his curls, and the pain eases off your heart and it feels softer. You see, my heart had got like a lump of stone with grief. . . .

"At first he used to ride with me while I drove the lorry, then I realized that that wouldn't do. What do I need when I'm on my own? A hunk of bread and an onion with a pinch of salt will last a soldier the whole day. But with him it's different. Now you've got to get him some milk, now you've got to boil an egg for him, and he can't get along without something hot. But I had my work to do. So I plucked up my courage and left him in the care of my friend's wife. Well, he just cried all day, and in the evening ran away to the elevator to meet me. Waited there till late at night.

"I had a hard time with him at first. After one very tiring day we went to bed when it was still light. He used to be always chirruping like a sparrow, but this time he was very quiet. 'What are you thinking about, son?' I asked. He just looks up at the ceiling and asks me: 'What did you do with your leather coat, Daddy?' And I'd never had a leather coat in my life! I had to get round it somehow. 'Left it in Voronezh,' I told him. 'And why were you so long looking for me?' So I said: 'I looked for you, sonny, in Germany, in Poland, and all over Byelorussia, and you turned up in Uryupinsk.' 'Is Uryupinsk nearer than Germany? Is it far from our house to Poland?' And so we went on talking till we dropped off to sleep.

"But do you think there wasn't a reason for his asking about that leather coat, mate? No, there was a reason behind it all right. It meant at some time or other his real father had worn a coat like that, and he had just remembered it. A kid's memory is like summer lightning, you know; it flashes and lights things up for a bit, then dies away. And that was how his memory worked, like the flashes of summer lightning.

"Mebbe we'd have gone on living another year in Uryupinsk together, but in November I had an accident. I was driving along a muddy road through a village and I went into a skid, and there happened to be a cow in the way and I knocked it over. Well, you know how it is, the women raised a hullabaloo, folk came crowding round, and soon there was a traffic inspector on the spot. I asked him to go easy, but he took my licence away. The cow got up, stuck its tail in the air and went galloping away down the street, but I lost my licence. I went through the winter as a joiner, and then got in touch with an old army friend —he works as a driver in our district—and he invited me to go and stay with him. You can do joinery work for a year, he says, then you can get a new licence in our region. So now my son and I, we're on the march to Kashary.

"But even if I hadn't had that accident with the cow, you know, I'd have left Uryupinsk just the same. My grief won't let me stay in one place for long. Now, when my Vanya gets older and he's got to be sent to school, then, mebbe, I'll knuckle under and settle down. But for the time being we're tramping the Russian land together."

"Does he get tired?" I asked.

"Well, he doesn't walk much on his own feet, most of the time he rides on me. I hoist him on to my shoulder and carry him, and if he wants to stretch his legs, he jumps down and runs about at the side of the road, prancing around like a little goat. All that wouldn't matter, mate, we'd get along all right, the only thing is my heart's got a knock in it somewhere, ought to have a piston changed. Sometimes it gives me such a stab I don't know what I'm doing. I'm afraid one day I may die in my sleep and frighten my little son. And then there's another trouble. Nearly every night I see in my dreams the dear ones I've lost. And mostly it's as if I was behind barbed wire and they were on the other side, at liberty. I talk about everything to Irina and the children, but as soon as I try to pull the barbed wire apart, they go away, seem to melt before my eyes. And there's another funny thing about it. In the daytime I always keep a firm grip on myself, you'll never get a sob or a sigh out of me, but sometimes I wake up at night and my pillow's wet with tears. . . ."

From the river came the sound of my friend's voice and the splash of oars in the water.

This stranger, who now seemed a close friend of mine, held out his big hand, firm as a block of wood:

"Good-bye, mate, good luck to you!"

"Good luck and a good journey to Kashary!"

"Thank you kindly. Heh, sonny, let's go to the boat."

The boy ran to his father's side, took hold of the corner of his quilted jacket and started off with tiny steps beside his striding father.

Two orphans, two grains of sand swept into strange parts by the tremendous hurricane of war.... What did the future hold for them? I wanted to believe that this Russian, this man of unbreakable will, would stick it out, and that the boy would grow at his father's side into a man who could endure anything, overcome any obstacle if his country called upon him to do so.

I felt sad as I watched them go. Perhaps everything would have been all right at our parting but for Vanya. After he had gone a few paces, he twisted round on his stumpy legs and waved to me with his little rosy hand. And suddenly a soft but taloned paw seemed to grip my heart, and I turned hastily away. No, not only in their sleep do they weep, these elderly men whose hair grew grey in the years of war. They weep, too, in their waking hours. The main thing is to be able to turn away in time. The really important thing is not to wound a child's heart, not to let him see that dry, burning tear on the cheek of a man.

1957

CPSIA information can be obtained at www.ICGtesting.com
Printed in the USA
LVOW040511150113

315748LV00002B/103/A

9 781410 104243